COMING ALIVE

THE SECOND WORLD WAR

WHAT IF THE BOMB GOES OFF?

STEWART ROSS

Illustrated by
LINDA CLARK

Evans

EVANS BROTHERS LIMITED

TO THE READER

What if the Bomb Goes Off? takes place in Britain during the early years of the Second World War. Bill Granger and the other characters in the book are made up, but the setting is real. The terrible bombing of Coventry in November 1940, for example, actually happened. So the story tells you what life was like during a dramatic period in our history.

Stewart Ross

For Springfield Primary School, Surrey.

Published by Evans Brothers Limited
2A Portman Mansions, Chiltern Street, London W1U 6NR

British Library Cataloguing in Publication Data
Ross, Stewart
What if the Bomb Goes Off? – (Coming alive)
1. World War, 1939-1945 – Social aspects – Great Britain – Juvenile fiction
2. Children's stories
I. Title
823.9'14(J)

Printed in Hong Kong

ISBN 0 237 52320 5

CONTENTS

THE BOMBERS ARE COMING!

DANGER

Britain entered the Second World War on 3 September 1939. Everyone knew that it would be different from previous wars. In the past, most British civilians had been safe from attack, but now enemy bombers could reach anywhere in the country.

POISON GAS

The government issued gas masks in case poison gas bombs were dropped. Air-raid shelters were built to protect city dwellers from bomb blasts. Important buildings were protected with sandbags. Hospitals, the police and fire services drew up emergency plans.

AIR RAIDS

At night, all street lights were switched off. Windows had to be blacked out to make it harder for enemy bombers to find their targets. Air-raid sirens sounded to warn people when an attack was expected. Wardens had the job of seeing that all these measures were carried out.

Despite the precautions, many people expected the big towns and cities to be reduced to rubble in a few weeks. In fact, things did not turn out quite like that.

PHONEY WAR

For the first eight months of the war, few enemy bombers appeared in the skies of Britain. Then suddenly, in May 1940, this 'Phoney War' ended. Adolf Hitler launched a massive attack on France and the Low Countries. The British army, fighting alongside the French, was defeated and the troops were brought home. Hitler conquered France and prepared to invade Britain...

CHAPTER ONE

SPECIAL MISSION

'War's great!' said Bill Granger, looking round at the rest of the gang.

Paul, Bill's ten-year-old brother, wasn't so sure. But he kept quiet. No one ever won an argument with Bill Granger.

William Horatio, known as Bill, wasn't a bully. He wasn't a particularly large twelve-year-old and there was nothing special about his untidy mouse-brown hair and bright grey-green eyes. What made him different was his brain.

Bill's brain picked up facts like a vacuum cleaner picks up dust. Except Bill's brain was never full. It was quick, too – quicker than any other brain in St Michael's Elementary School, Coventry. Bill worked out the answers to Mrs Matthews' mental arithmetic tests faster than any pupil she had ever taught.

So when Bill said the war was great, Paul said nothing. The other members of the Radford Road Gang – Dennis Smith and Charlie Boxer – didn't say anything, either. Dennis, a tall, gangly boy the same age as Bill, never spoke much anyway. Bill called him 'the strong, silent type' ('SST' for short). The eleven-year-old Charlie (or 'Perky', another of Bill's nicknames) just grinned. Nothing upset Charlie. At least, not then. When he was teased for wearing his elder brother's hand-me-down trousers, three sizes too big for him, he just laughed and said, 'Better than going naked, eh?'

•   •   •   •   •

It was a hot afternoon in the middle of the summer holidays, 1940. All four members of the Radford Road Gang were sitting with their legs dangling over the edge of the canal. As usual, they were talking about the war. 'Don't you want to know why it's great?' prompted Bill.

'Why's the war great?' asked Charlie, staring into the murky waters of the canal and wondering how fish survived in such a filthy soup.

'Well,' said Bill, warming to his subject, 'we've got more freedom for a start,' he explained.

It was true, the others realised. Because of the war, their parents were either away from home or at work all day, and the boys had all the time in the world to get on with their own business.

Bill's dad was a fitter with the RAF in East Anglia and his mum had recently taken a full-time job at the Daimler factory, making armoured cars. Dennis' dad was in the army, and his mum was always out doing voluntary work. Charlie didn't have a dad. Not one that he had met, anyway. He didn't have much of a mum, either – she worked behind the bar of the Lady Godiva and didn't get home until almost midnight. Sometimes, Charlie said, she didn't come home at all.

After giving everyone time to think through what he had said, Bill went on. 'The war's exciting, too.'

Again, he waited for someone to ask what he meant. Eventually, Paul obliged.

'What d'you mean?' he yawned. 'It's not very exciting staring into a stinky old canal, is it?'

Bill leaned back and closed his eyes. With the sun full on his face, he felt dreamy – almost inspired. 'Listen, Paul,' he said. 'This is just the rest period. The Radford Road Gang is gathering its strength, preparing for a special mission.'

'What special mission?' asked Paul, suddenly feeling more awake.

Bill sat up. '*Sssh!* Not so loud, Paul. Come closer, all of you.'

When the gang had gathered around him, Bill explained, 'Coventry's top secret, you know, with loads of factories making weapons. So why have we had only a few air raids?' Bill looked at the blank faces around him, then answered himself. 'Because Jerry wants to find out about those weapons, not blow them up. And how's he going to find out?'

The others shrugged their shoulders.

'Spies!' whispered Bill. '*German spies!* The city's teeming with them.'

Dennis scratched his head. 'OK. But I still don't get where we fit in.'

Bill's eyes shone with enthusiasm. 'Come on, SST! It's our job to track them down. That's our special mission – *a spy hunt!*'

Chapter two

THE SUSPECT

Bill's idea lifted the gang's spirits. They had spent the first weeks of the holidays plane-spotting and fighting mock battles. Their only adventure had been when Paul fell into the canal pretending to be a soldier at Dunkirk. Now, at last, they were going to do something really important.

Back in the kitchen of the Grangers' house in Abbotts Lane, the Radford Road Gang made plans.

'Order Number One: I vote we hunt in groups of two,' said Bill. 'Paul and I will be A Group, and Perky and SST will be B Group. That way we'll be less obvious. Those in favour of Order Number One, raise a hand.'

Each gang member dutifully raised a hand.

'Order Number Two,' Bill went on. 'I vote we do two searches a day, one in the morning and one in the afternoon. We report back to base after each one.'

'Er, where's base?' asked Paul.

'Here, of course,' said Bill. 'Right, those in favour of Order Number Two, raise a hand.'

Again, the gang members raised their hands.

'Now, let's work out our sectors,' Bill continued. Bringing a street map from the living-room, he divided the city in half with his finger. 'A Group has the west sector and B Group the east, OK?'

'What's a "sector"?' asked Charlie, staring at the map in confusion.

'It's the army word for a piece of land,' Bill explained.

'Oh…' muttered Charlie, none the wiser.

Bill folded up the map and said dramatically, 'OK, Radford Road Gang, we start at dawn! Any more questions?'

Dennis scratched his head. 'Er, yes. How do we recognise one of these spies?'

'Easy!' Bill explained, standing up and leaning against the stove. 'Look out for three things. One: suspicious behaviour, such as eavesdropping. Two: suspicious looks. All Jerries are blonde and wear leather clothes. Three: suspicious accents. Even the best educated Jerries don't sound English. Got it, SST?'

Dennis nodded wisely.

Charlie wasn't so sure. 'Adolf Hitler isn't blonde,' he said quietly.

Bill sighed. 'Adolf Hitler used to live in Austria, Perky.'

'Ah!' muttered Charlie, wondering if his fair hair would turn black if he, too, went to live in Austria.

The Radford Road Gang spent the rest of the holidays patrolling the streets of Coventry. The boys listened at queues outside greengrocers', hung around bus stops and, once, with Charlie's mum's permission, hid behind the bar of the Lady Godiva to hear what the drinkers were saying. But it was all in vain. Not once did they spot anyone who looked or sounded even vaguely like a spy.

When the autumn term started, they cut their patrols to one a day, beginning after school and finishing when it got dark. Evening was the best time for spy-hunting, Bill assured them, because spies hated the light.

Eventually, a few weeks later, he was proved right.

It was Dennis who saw him first – a tall, fair-haired man in a leather jacket going into the Gaumont Cinema. B Group crossed the road and reached the foyer in time to hear the suspect buying his ticket. His accent was definitely not English.

When B Group reported their findings back at base, Bill immediately ordered a 'recce' (army slang for a closer look, he explained). The Radford Road Gang piled out of the house and headed towards the cinema.

'Hey! You kids! Where do you think you're going?'

The gang turned to find Mr Peters, the local air-raid warden bearing down on them.

'What are you doing out now?' he asked, drawing level with them. 'And where are your gas masks? Get back indoors before I call the police!'

The gang returned to the Grangers' and slumped miserably around the kitchen table.

'Stupid man!' muttered Bill. 'He's probably just lost us the war. Who needs wardens? We've only had a few raids. Anyway, Jerry's not going to blitz Coventry, is he? Not with his own spies here.'

The gang resumed its search after school the next day, but without success. The spy was nowhere to be seen.

As the weeks slipped by without another sighting, Bill and Paul began to wonder whether B Group's spy really existed.

CHAPTER THREE

BLITZ

Mrs Granger did not like leaving Bill and Paul alone at night and she normally swapped her late shifts at the factory with a neighbour, Mr Lambert. But on the evening of 15 November, Mr Lambert was unwell. Mrs Granger gave Bill and Paul their tea, and asked Mrs Lambert to call in from time to time to make sure they were all right. Then she left to catch the 5.39 p.m. bus for the factory.

'Make sure you get down to the cellar double-quick if the siren goes off, and don't forget your gas masks!' she had called as she opened the front door to leave. 'Sleep well, boys! I'll be back before you wake up.'

As she closed the front door behind her, she was surprised to find the city bathed in bright, clear moonlight.

Bill and Paul were sitting on the living-room floor building a Meccano crane when the air-raid siren sounded.

Paul immediately jumped to his feet. 'Quick, Bill! Let's get down to the cellar.'

Bill stayed where he was. 'No hurry, Paul,' he muttered. 'Probably just a practice.'

Paul went upstairs to fetch their gas masks. When he came back, Bill was still working on the crane. 'Come on, Bill!' Paul pleaded.

'Keep your hair on, Paul! Jerry can wait a bit.'

Paul crossed the room, pushed aside the black-out curtain and opened the window. From far away to the east came the low drone of aircraft.

'Bill!' he yelled, rushing back into the room. 'It's not a practice! It's real!'

'Oh, yes?' said Bill without looking up. Then he paused. 'What's that noise?'

'I told you! *It's bombers!*' cried Paul, almost in tears.

The sound had swelled into an ominous roar. The living-room windows began to rattle. 'Blimey!' shouted Bill, throwing the Meccano back in its box. 'Come on, A Group, let's get out of here!'

Clutching their gas masks, the boys stumbled down the wooden steps into the cellar just as the first bombs started to fall.

Wave after wave of aircraft came over the city that night, growling like angry dogs. The eerie whistle of the bombs that fell from their black

underbellies rose to a screech as they neared the ground. Then silence, followed moments later by the long, angry 'crump' of explosion.

Lying together on the cellar floor, trembling with fear, Bill and Paul listened in silence to the dreadful destruction going on around them. Occasionally, a bomb fell quite close, shaking the house and sending clouds of dust tumbling from the rafters overhead.

After about an hour, the candle Bill had lit burned out. He was too frightened to search for another.

When the all-clear sounded just before dawn, the boys lay lost in their own thoughts for a while. Eventually, Paul asked quietly, 'Do you think anyone else is alive, Bill?'

'I hope so,' his brother replied. He began fumbling on the floor for the matches.

'What about Mum?'

'She'll be OK, Paul. There's a big shelter near the factory.'

Bill struck a match, found a spare candle and lit it. A flickering yellow light lit up the cellar.

Paul stared at his brother. 'You look like a ghost,' he said with a shiver. He hadn't realised till now how cold it was.

'What do you mean?' asked Bill.

'You're all covered in dust.'

Bill smiled. 'You could do with a bath yourself.'

After another long silence, Paul asked, 'Did you mean what you said about Mum being OK?'

'Of course.'

'But you're not always right, are you, Bill?' said Paul.

'What do you mean?'

Paul began brushing the dust off his face. 'In the holidays you said the war was great...'

When Bill didn't reply, he added, 'And you said that Jerry wouldn't blitz Coventry.'

Bill looked at his brother for a moment, then lowered his eyes. 'I was wrong, Paul. I'm sorry,' he said quietly.

CHAPTER FOUR

BOMB DAMAGE

'You boys all right down there?' called Mrs Lambert from the top of the cellar steps.

Hearing an adult voice, Bill and Paul felt less miserable.

'OK, thanks, Mrs Lambert!' Bill replied, scrambling to his feet and offering a hand to Paul.

The boys cheered up even more when Mrs Lambert told them that everyone in the Daimler factory shelter was safe and Mrs Granger was on her way home.

'She won't be back quite yet, though,' she explained. 'She's got to walk, poor thing. There ain't no buses nor trams nor anything at the moment. The city took quite a knock last night.'

'Quite a knock' was an understatement.

On their way next door for breakfast, the boys stopped and looked about them. They had seen pictures of the London Blitz in the papers, so they knew what bombing could do. But that was just photographs. This was real, with all the sounds and smells of a city that had had its heart torn out.

Apart from a few broken windows, the Grangers' and the Lamberts' houses weren't badly damaged. But the rest of Abbotts Lane was in a terrible state.

The pavements were strewn with bits of brick, wood and glass. The street lamps, as upright as soldiers the night before, leaned sideways like the drinkers leaving the Lady Godiva.

The front of number twenty-four had been blown away so you could see straight into the rooms, like a dolls' house. Outside there was a huge dark hole in the road. Watched by a small crowd, fire-fighters were tackling a blaze in the bakery near the Radford Road. From time to time, shouted instructions rose above the hiss of the water and the roar of the flames.

At number sixteen, where Paul's friend Neville Walker lived, a rescue team was searching through the rubble for survivors. Beyond them, in the direction of the cathedral, the smoke from a dozen fires curled into the drizzly sky. A sharp, sickly smell of burning hung in the still air.

Mrs Granger, pale and exhausted, arrived home in the middle of the morning and took the boys back home. She bought sandwiches and tea from a mobile canteen for lunch. Finally, after sweeping up the glass and pinning bits of cardboard over the broken windows, they all slept.

● ● ● ● ●

Although the sirens went off a couple of times, the bombers did not return for a while. Mrs Granger stayed at home for three days while the factory was being repaired.

It was too dangerous for the boys to go out, so they hung about the house reading and playing

cards. On the fourth day, hearing that school was re-opening that morning, Mrs Granger returned to work.

The boys walked down the road with her, then said goodbye and headed for school. Some tidying up had already been done. A few buses were running again and in some streets the only reminder of the Blitz was an ugly gap where a house had once stood.

St Michael's Elementary School looked unharmed. However, on the locked gates hung a sign: CLOSED UNTIL FURTHER NOTICE. Looking up, the boys saw a gaping hole in the roof.

'Mum must have got it wrong,' said Bill, who had been looking forward to swapping stories about the Blitz with his friends.

Turning to leave, they saw Dennis loping towards them like a baby giraffe. 'Hey! You two!' he shouted. 'Wait!'

'School's shut,' called Paul.

'I know!' Dennis puffed, resting his hands on his knees to get his breath back. 'But listen – I've seen him – again!'

'Seen who?' asked Bill.

'The spy, of course!' cried Dennis. 'He's down by Spon Street, snooping about and writing things down in a notebook!'

CHAPTER FIVE

EVIDENCE

Dennis explained that he had spotted the spy while doing some shopping for his mum. He had trailed him as far as Spon Street, where the man had inspected several ruined houses and then written something in a notebook. Worried that his mum would wonder where he'd got to, Dennis had decided to return home. He had come via the school in the hope of meeting Bill and Paul.

'Good work, SST!' said Bill. Now the shock of the Blitz was wearing off, he sounded more like his old self. 'A Group will take over. You get your shopping done, then contact Perky and come round to base at fourteen-hundred hours.'

'When?' asked Dennis.

'Fourteen-hundred hours – that's two o'clock in army talk.'

'Right,' said Dennis. 'I'll see you at base at fourteen… er, two o'clock. 'Bye!' He strode off, leaving Bill and Paul to continue the mission.

Paul was worried. 'You know we're not playing at war any more, Bill,' he said nervously. 'I mean, shouldn't we just tell the police?'

Bill shook his head. 'They wouldn't believe us. We need *evidence*. And this is *not* a game. This is a real operation that could help win the war.'

Paul was still not sure. Nevertheless, he went along with his brother to see what would happen. After all, he told himself, there was no harm in just going to look at the spy, was there?

When Bill and Paul reached Spon Street, they found the damage much worse than around Abbotts Lane. Few of the buildings on either side of the deserted street were still intact. From the blackened timbers and scorched bricks, it was clear that there had been a number of fires.

Paul shuddered. 'It's like a graveyard, Bill. It gives me the creeps.'

But Bill wasn't listening. His eyes were fixed on a tall man standing on the pavement at the end of the street. In his left hand he held a small notebook.

'It's him!' hissed Bill, pushing Paul back against the front wall of an abandoned pub. 'Look, the leather jacket! And the notebook!'

As they watched, the spy took out a pencil and started writing.

'What's he doing?' asked Paul.

'He's assessing the damage,' Bill whispered. 'He'll probably report back to the *Luftwaffe*.' He fished an old exercise book out his pocket. 'Now, we must write down our evidence.'

Paul hadn't taken his eyes off the spy for a moment. Suddenly, he gave a muffled yell, 'Look out! He's coming this way!'

Sure enough, the spy had finished taking notes and was walking quickly towards the boys.

'Follow me!' said Bill. He grabbed Paul by the hand and dashed through the broken doorway of the pub.

The inside smelt of beer and ashes. The boys hurried across the carpet of broken glass, through an opening behind the bar and into a sort of kitchen. Hearts pounding, they ducked down behind an overturned table.

When it was clear that they hadn't been followed, the boys got up and looked around. The grey November sky was clearly visible through a large hole in the ceiling. Beneath it, the floor had collapsed. Edging cautiously towards the opening, they found themselves looking down into the pub's cellar. There, its point embedded in the tiled floor, was the unmistakable shape of a large bomb.

'Cripes!' said Paul softly. '*It's huge!*'

'It hasn't – gone off – but it might,' said Bill, speaking very deliberately. 'Turn round – Paul – and walk – to the door. Try not – to disturb – anything.' Taking one step at a time, the boys retreated to the street.

'Now what?' asked Paul.

Bill wasn't sure. To cover his confusion, he announced, 'This is a matter for the whole gang, Paul. We must report to base at once.'

CHAPTER SIX

'DARE YOU!'

From the moment Charlie took his seat at the Grangers' kitchen table, it was clear that something was wrong. He sat there, hands stuffed into his pockets, saying nothing. Eventually, Dennis asked him what the matter was.

'Don't want to be in the gang no more. It's stupid!' he replied, staring at the tablecloth.

'What do you mean, Perky?' asked Bill. He was upset. No one had ever called his ideas stupid before.

Charlie explained that during the Blitz, when he was sitting in a shelter with his mum, he had told her about the spy. She had said there weren't any spies. And even if there were, it wasn't for kids to go looking for them. War wasn't a game, she said. It was real – and horrible. Charlie knew she was telling the truth because when he came out of the shelter, he saw dead bodies. All twisted and covered in blood.

The gang was shocked and embarrassed by what Charlie had said. They knew that his mum was right, too.

'I said we should go to the police,' muttered Paul.

'We will, when we've got the evidence,' Bill explained firmly.

Charlie lifted his head. 'You and your daft evidence, Bill Granger!' he said angrily. 'You think it's some sort of science lesson, don't you!'

'*Rubbish!*' Bill replied huffily. 'Anyway, Paul and I have something more important to tell you.'

'Oh, yes?' scoffed Charlie.

'Yes. We've found a bomb. A real one.'

He told the rest of the gang how they had seen the spy at work and found the unexploded bomb at the back of the pub.

Charlie didn't believe him. There weren't such things as unexploded bombs, he said. They always went off – he'd heard them. The one in

35

the pub was probably just a wooden dummy that Jerry had dropped to frighten people. 'You're wrong, Bill,' he continued. 'You were wrong about Coventry not being blitzed. And you're wrong about this bomb.'

'*I'm not!*' shouted Bill, close to tears. 'I'll prove it!'

'How?'

'I'll go back and fetch a bit of metal from it.'

'All right. You do that, Bill Granger. And if it really is metal, then I'll believe you.'

'You shouldn't have said that, Bill,' said Paul when Dennis and Charlie had gone. 'It was silly, wasn't it?'

Bill was still angry. In his heart, he knew that his brother was right. He'd been as scared as Paul when they first found the bomb, but he didn't want to admit it. Besides, he was sure about one thing – a wooden dummy wouldn't bury itself in the ground like that. Once he had shown that Charlie was wrong, he would tell the police about the bomb and the spy.

'All right, Paul,' he said. 'You've made your point. But that bomb is real and I'm going to prove it.'

'That's daft, Bill,' Paul cried. 'It'll go off if you touch it.'

'It didn't go off when it came though the roof, did it? Anyway, I won't touch it. I'll find a bit of tail fin or something that's fallen off.'

'Someone'll see you,' said Paul, desperately trying to put his brother off.

'They won't. I'll sneak out at night.' Then he said something else he knew he shouldn't. 'You coming with me? *Dare you!*'

'You're my brother,' Paul replied quietly. 'Suppose I'll have to.'

Bill and Paul crept out of the house around midnight. It was raining and the streets were dark and deserted. Even the air-raid wardens had given up on their black-out patrols and had gone home to bed.

Sticking to side-streets, the boys made their way quickly to Spon Street. The place was even more sinister at night, thought Paul.

As he crept along behind his brother, the black windows of the bombed-out buildings stared down on him like eyes in an empty skull.

CHAPTER SEVEN

TRAPPED

The bomb was still there, sticking into the floor of the cellar like a huge grey dart. Bill shone his torch around it.

'What's that?' he whispered, fixing the beam on a piece of twisted metal.

Paul moved carefully towards the hole to get a better look. 'Dunno. Just a bit of old iron.'

'Bet it came from the bomb. I'll go and get it.' Bill flashed the torch around the room. 'There's a door over there. I reckon it's the way down. You hang on here. Back in a minute.'

He stumbled across the room towards the doorway, then disappeared from sight.

Paul shuddered, and not just from the cold. What if there was a dead body still in the pub, buried under the rubble? What if he was standing on it without realising? The hairs on the back of his neck rose in terror...

'*Bill!*' he cried.

'Yes?' came a muffled reply.

'Come back! Please!'

Seconds later, the friendly light of the torch reappeared in the doorway. 'What do you want?'

'I'm scared, Bill. Let's go home.'

Bill came over and put a hand on Paul's arm.

'Yes, it's quite spooky, isn't it?' he said. What's worse, the stairs to the cellar are blocked off. I can't get down that way.'

'So can we go home now?' asked Paul.

Bill shone the torch back towards the bomb. 'Maybe we'll have to…' At that moment, the torch beam rested on some writing stencilled on to the side of the bomb.

'Hang on!' cried Bill. 'That's the serial number! If I can get that, it'll prove it's real.' He edged towards the opening.

Neither of the boys was quite sure what happened next. There was a cracking noise beneath Bill's feet. Sliding towards the hole, he grabbed at Paul to steady himself. There was another crack. Paul screamed. The floor gave way and both boys fell heavily into the cellar.

Bill lost consciousness when his head crashed on to the hard tiles of the cellar's floor. When he came round, he heard Paul crying in the darkness somewhere to his left.

'You OK, Paul?' he whispered.

The crying stopped. He heard a sharp intake of breath. 'Is that you, Bill?'

'Who else?'

41

'I thought you were dead! What happened?'

'I think I was knocked out. My head hurts. I can't see anything. Ow! My arm hurts, too.'

'I've hurt my ankle,' wailed Paul. 'Where are you? I want to go home!'

The torch had broken when they fell. Guided by their voices, the boys crawled towards each other in the blackness. When they met, they checked their injuries. Paul had a twisted ankle and couldn't walk. Bill had a splitting headache and felt dizzy when he tried to stand.

Paul began to cry again. 'What are we going to do, Bill?' he sobbed. 'What if the bomb goes off?'

'It won't. It's not a time bomb.'

'How do you know?'

'Because it's not ticking. Listen…'

It had started to rain and the only sound was the steady drip of water from the broken edge of the floor above them.

'Look, we'll shout for help. Someone'll hear us.' Bill took a deep breath and yelled. *'He-e-e-elp!'*

To his horror, instead of bringing help, the vibrations of his shout dislodged a cascade of plaster and broken tiles from the floor above. Some of it clanged against the sides of the bomb.

'That was a close shave!' said Bill when the avalanche had finally stopped. 'We'd better not do that again. We might set off the bomb.'

'What now?' asked Paul weakly.

Bill sighed. 'I don't know, Paul. We're trapped, aren't we?'

42

CHAPTER EIGHT

THE SPY

Bill felt utterly wretched. He had let down his mum, who would be frantic when she found out that they were missing. He felt terrible about Paul, too, and wished that he'd never dared him to come.

Trying to make up for his foolishness, Bill made his brother comfortable and did his best to cheer him up. He made jokes and told Bible stories, even adding details of his own. As he was explaining exactly how David cut off Goliath's head, he realised that Paul had dozed off. Soon afterwards, utterly exhausted, Bill drifted into a deep sleep himself.

Half awake, Paul reached for his blankets. They weren't there. Slowly, the memory of the previous night returned. Praying he'd been dreaming, he opened his eyes. In daylight the bomb looked more grim and menacing than ever.

Now fully awake, Paul became aware of men talking in the street outside. He woke Bill and for a couple of minutes they listened to what was being said. A man was giving orders. He talked about 'starting with the roof.' All of a sudden, Bill realised with horror what was happening.

The ruined pub was about to be demolished. Obviously, the workmen hadn't seen the unexploded bomb in the cellar or the terrified boys lying on the damp floor beside it.

'We've got to let them know we're here,' Bill croaked. 'If they start knocking the roof in, we'll be buried alive or the bomb will go off and that'll be the end of everyone!'

Paul felt sick. 'But if we start shouting again—'

'We've got to,' interrupted Bill. 'Best not to think about it. On the count of three, OK?' Paul gave a feeble nod. 'Right. One... two... three...'

Hearing the boys' yells, the head of the demolition gang entered the pub. In the kitchen he peered through the broken floor at what looked like two partly buried statues. A fresh avalanche of debris had covered the boys' legs

and part of their bodies. The bomb, covered with dust and fallen debris, was almost unrecognisable.

'Anyone there?' called the man.

'Yes!' croaked Bill, spitting out a mouthful of dust.

'Hang on you two! We'll be with you in a jiffy.'

'*No!*' Bill cried. 'On the right. It's a bomb.'

The man looked down into the hole. 'I don't believe it!' he whispered. 'Don't move an inch. I'll be right back.'

The rescue team cleared the cellar stairs and carried Bill and Paul out on stretchers. The area was then evacuated and the bomb disposal team moved in. They confirmed that the object in the cellar was indeed an unexploded bomb and spent the rest of the morning making it safe.

The boys were taken to hospital, where they were joined by their mother. She was so relieved to find them safe that she didn't question them too closely about their disappearance. That, thought Bill ominously, would come later.

• • • • •

In the middle of the afternoon a man in a leather coat entered the ward and started walking towards Bill and Paul.

'Look, Bill!' gasped Paul. *'It's the spy!'*

'Sister says I can ask a few questions,' the man began, speaking in a strange accent. 'Don't mind, do you?'

'You're a spy!' Paul blurted out. 'I'm not telling you anything!'

'Spy?' laughed the stranger. 'I'm Jake Dawson, a reporter for *The Sydney Star*, Australia. I'm writing about how the Old Country is coping with the Blitz. I'd like to do a piece on you two – something like 'Schoolboy Heroes…

'*Heroes?*' Bill repeated wide-eyed. He wondered if Mr Dawson was laughing at them.

'Why not? If you hadn't found the bomb, a lot of people would have been killed. Mind you, I'd like to know what you were doing down there in the first place. So are you going to tell me?'

'I'll try,' grinned Bill, 'but you won't believe it.'

The home front

AIR-RAID SHELTERS

Bill and Paul Granger sheltered from the Blitz in the cellar of their home. Cellars were fairly safe, but people sheltering in them could be trapped or killed if the building above collapsed. The Walkers, who were sheltering in the cellar of number sixteen, Abbotts Lane, were killed when their house received a direct hit. Some people, like Charlie and his mother, sheltered in large concrete air-raid shelters. Others went to corrugated iron shelters (known as Morrison Shelters) put up in their gardens. These gave protection only if high-explosive bombs landed some distance away.

BLACKOUT

Mr Peters, the ARP (Air-Raid Protection) warden who looked after Abbotts Lane, made sure that no lights were visible from the street. Most people blacked out their windows with heavy curtains.

WAR WORK

In May 1939, when the government introduced 'conscription' for men, Mr Granger joined the RAF and Mr Smith joined the army. In March 1941, the government said that young women had to be prepared to do war work. Before that, women were encouraged to do work that would help with the war effort. That's why Mrs Granger, who had been a housewife before the war, went to work in the Daimler factory. Mrs Smith's voluntary work was with the WVS (Women's Voluntary Service). The mobile canteens that brought round food and drinks after the Coventry Blitz were run by the WVS.

DUNKIRK

In May 1940, a sudden German attack in France drove the British, French and Belgian armies back towards the Channel. They gathered on the beaches near the port of Dunkirk and the British government asked everyone with sea-going boats to help rescue them. Remarkably, the fleet of warships and small boats managed to pick up more than 330,000 men and bring them back to Britain.

THE LONDON BLITZ

After the defeat of France in June 1940, Hitler prepared to invade Britain. First, he had to gain control of the skies. This led to a series of air battles during the summer of 1940, known as the Battle of Britain. The *Luftwaffe* failed to wipe out the RAF, the invasion was postponed, and in

September the Germans tried to take Britain out of the war by devastating London with air raids. These raids, which lasted until May 1941, were known as the Blitz. Over 54,000 tonnes of bombs were dropped, 40,000 people were killed and over a million homes were destroyed. Nevertheless, the Blitz did not break British morale or seriously disrupt industrial production.

THE COVENTRY BLITZ

Between June and October 1940 the *Luftwaffe* carried out several small raids on Coventry, killing over 200 people. By far the biggest raid – the Coventry Blitz, which the Germans code-named 'Operation Moonlight Sonata' – began at about 7.30 p.m. on 15 November and lasted most of the night. Bombers dropped 30,000 incendiary bombs, 500 tonnes of high explosive and various other devices intended to start fires. The effect was devastating – 4,330 homes were destroyed and 554 men, women and children were killed. A further 865 people were injured. At one time there were over 200 separate fires in the city and the blaze could be seen by approaching aircraft over 200 kilometres away. For several days most homes were without gas, water and electricity supplies. At the time, it was the worst raid on a single city the world had ever seen.

NEW WORDS

Air raid An attack by enemy aircraft, usually bombers.

Air-raid shelter A place where people could shelter from a bomb attack. Many were underground. They were usually made of steel or concrete.

Blackout Making sure no lights on the ground could be seen from the air. The blackout was enforced to make it difficult for enemy bombers to find their target.

Blitz The heavy bombing of a city. 'Blitz' comes from the German word *Blitzkrieg* which means 'lightning war'.

Casualty Someone who's injured or wounded.

Civilian Someone not in the army, navy or air force.

Conscription Compulsory service in the armed forces.

Elementary school The name given to primary and junior schools. Until after the Second World War, most children had only elementary schooling.

Fitter A type of engineer.

Incendiary bomb A bomb designed to start a fire when it lands.

Jerry A slang word for a German, used in the Second World War.

Low Countries Belgium and the Netherlands.

Luftwaffe The German air force.

Meccano A metal construction toy.

Phoney War The name the British gave to the period of September 1939 – May 1940, when there was little fighting in Western Europe.

Recce (pronounced 'recky') This is army slang for 'reconnaissance', which means to keep a situation under observation.

Rubble Broken bricks, slates and tiles.

Sandbag A cloth bag filled with sand.

Warden Someone who looks after others. An air raid warden, for example, helped people during air raids.

• • • • •

TIME LINE

1936 Britain starts building air-raid shelters.

1939 **September** War begins. Blackout started.
First air raids over southern England.

1940 **May** German forces invade France
and the Low Countries.
May–June British army rescued from
Dunkirk.
25 June Coventry first bombed.
July–September Battle of Britain.
September London Blitz begins (ends
May 1941).
15 November Coventry Blitz.

1941 **March** Women have to sign up to do
war work.
April Two more heavy raids on Coventry.
December USA joins the war.

1942 **August** Last of forty-one air raids on
Coventry.

1944 **July** Missiles hit London.

1945 **May** War ends in Europe.
August War ends in Far East.

1962 New cathedral opened in Coventry,
replacing the medieval one destroyed in
the Blitz of 1940.